A Merry Christmas Rhyme

―――― **Paul Haughey** ――――

Illustrations by Dwain Esper

AuthorHouse™ UK Ltd.
1663 Liberty Drive
Bloomington, IN 47403 USA
www.authorhouse.co.uk
Phone: 0800.197.4150

© 2013 Paul Haughey. All Rights Reserved.

No part of this book may be reproduced, stored in a retrieval system,
or transmitted by any means without the written permission of the author.

Published by AuthorHouse 06/24/2013

ISBN: 978-1-4817-8609-6 (sc)
978-1-4817-8610-2 (e)

Any people depicted in stock imagery provided by Thinkstock are models,
and such images are being used for illustrative purposes only.
Certain stock imagery © Thinkstock.

Because of the dynamic nature of the Internet, any web addresses or links contained in this book may have changed since publication and may no longer be valid. The views expressed in this work are solely those of the author and do not necessarily reflect the views of the publisher, and the publisher hereby disclaims any responsibility for them.

authorHOUSE®

In a time before time
Before memories can start
There lived an old wizard
Called Merlin Braveheart

        He stood tall and thin
        With a very long beard
        And most of the neighbours
        Thought Merlin was weird

                He lived by himself
                With an old tawny owl
                And drank magic potions
                That tasted quite foul

He worked all day long
But each night left his cavern
To go down the street
For a drink in the tavern

        He brought with him his owl
        His name was Night-night
        And perched on his shoulder
        The two were a sight

Merlin drank soda
But Night-Night drank beer
(He didn't like spirits
they made him feel queer)

        They sat in a corner
        on an old wooden chair
        and to strangers at least
        they seemed an odd pair

                Merlin spoke not a word
                Save to order his drink
                Then sat in the corner
                To ponder and think

He would stroke his long beard
And into space stare
So that those in the tavern
Were all unaware

        That Merlin was listening
        To all that they said
        The jobs that they did
        How much they were paid

The price of potatoes
The cost of a loaf
He could tell who was clever
And who was an oaf

        And who was a good man
        And who was a thief
        And those that got into
        A little mischief

                For men tend to talk
                When they've been drinking
                So Merlin sat quiet
                Listening and thinking

Of how he could help
Those folk most in need
Though none that he helped
Knew of his creed

7

Tom Timber the carpenter
Had such a hard life
With six scrawny children
And a very ill wife

        He worked all day long
        So when they went to bed
        Down the street for a night cap
        To the the tavern he'd head

                But only one drink
                Could Tom Timber afford
                But even for that
                He would thank the Good Lord

Tom worked with wood
And needed some more
But only one piece
Had he left in the store

        But Merlin worked magic
        And the wood it just grew
        So when Tim took a piece
        It itself would renew

Tom was delighted
Worked hard with the wood
And soon all his children
Enjoyed lots of food

        His wife she grew stronger
        Her health did return
        But where his luck came from
        He never would learn

                At times in the tavern
                On his luck he would think
                And one night Merlin's owl
                At Tom Timber did wink

He knew that this gesture
Was both strange and funny
Perhaps it was Merlin
Who made him his money

        But Merlin said nothing
        So Tom never knew
        It was Merlin who made
        Tom's dreams come true

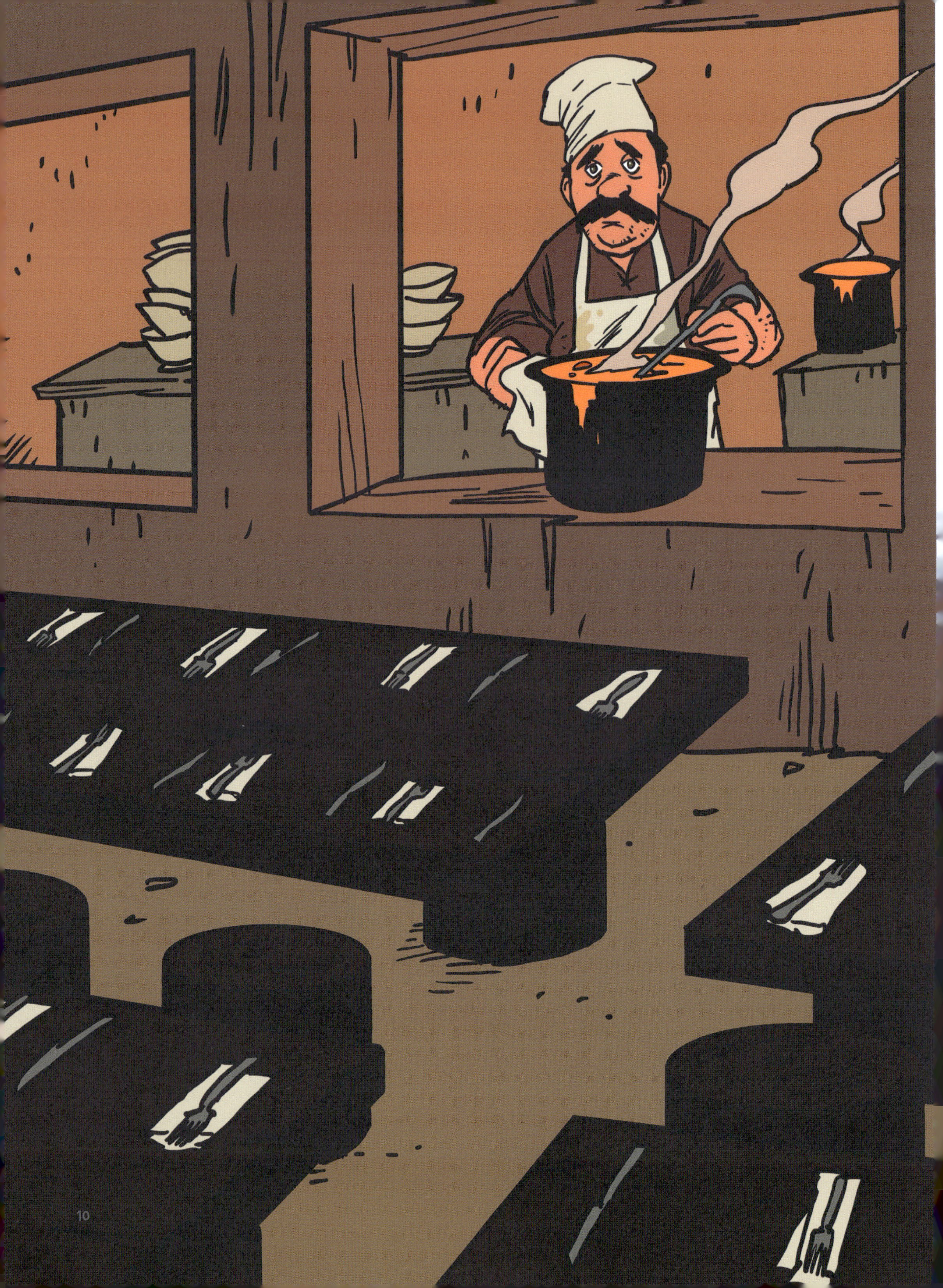

Bill Boyle was a cook
Who got into trouble
Food poisoning, unfortunately
Burst Bill Boyle's bubble

        A few years ago
        He had all you could want
        So successful was he
        In his fine restaurant

                But then, just one time
                He didn't take care
                The cooked and the raw meat
                To divide and prepare

Now this little bug
They call salmonella
Is what you would call
A real nasty fella

        The people who ate
        In the restaurant that night
        For the next seven days
        Had a terrible plight

From toilet to bed
They would hop, skip and jump
And the Docs were compelled
Their stomachs to pump

        The word got around
        Bill Boyle was to blame
        For his catering business
        The end it soon came

                Bill Boyle then lost heart
                And started to slink
                To the tavern where Merlin
                And Night-Night did drink

So Merlin invented
A burger so fine
That made one feel giggly
And bubbly, like wine

        And best thing of all
        An ingredient put in
        Made the person who ate
        The burger - grow thin

The secret to make
This great recipe
Was made up by Merlin
To help Bill you see

        It was posted by Night-Night
        Through Bill Boyle's front door
        When folk tasted the burgers
        They came back for more

                In no time at all
                Bill Boyle had grown rich
                Whilst before Merlin helped him
                He hadn't a stitch

But Bill always wondered
Who changed his lot
But try as he might
Find out - he could not

        He once asked the wizard
        In the tavern one night
        But the wizard just smiled
        And so did Night-Night

14

Will Waxxle made candles
But not very well
The wicks burnt too quickly
So few could he sell

        His family was large
        And his parents were poor
        So he struggled to keep
        The wolf from the door

                If no candles were sold
                His spirits would sink
                And poor Willie Waxxle
                Would turn to the drink

And there he would stand
At the end of the bar
And tell all the drinkers
From near and afar

        Whether they wished
        Or wanted to know
        They just had to listen
        To Wee Willie's woe

Of course Merlin was listening
And decided at last
To help Willie Waxxle
Some magic he'd cast

        The following morning
        When Will Waxxle arose
        He looked down and he saw
        Something tied to his toes

                On closer inspection
                It turned out a note
                Though he never found out
                The person who wrote

The message that read
'This is no trick
Just do what I say
To fashion your wick'

        The instructions he followed
        Right to the letter
        And the candles he made
        Were not alone better

No matter how long
The candle would burn
No change on the wick
Could people discern

           It never burned out
           Just lasted for ever
           An infinite candle
           Now wasn't that clever!

                      People would say
                      (Though it sounds somewhat silly)
                      That no one could hold
                      A candle to Willie

The more he grew rich
The less did he care
How the note on his toe
Had come to be there

          Though one night in the tavern
          When he'd had too much beer
          He teased poor old Merlin
          Whom he thought somewhat queer

He challenged the wizard
To conjure a trick
That could ever compare
With Will Waxxle's wick

But Merlin just smiled
And then glanced away
That he'd worked the magic
He never would say

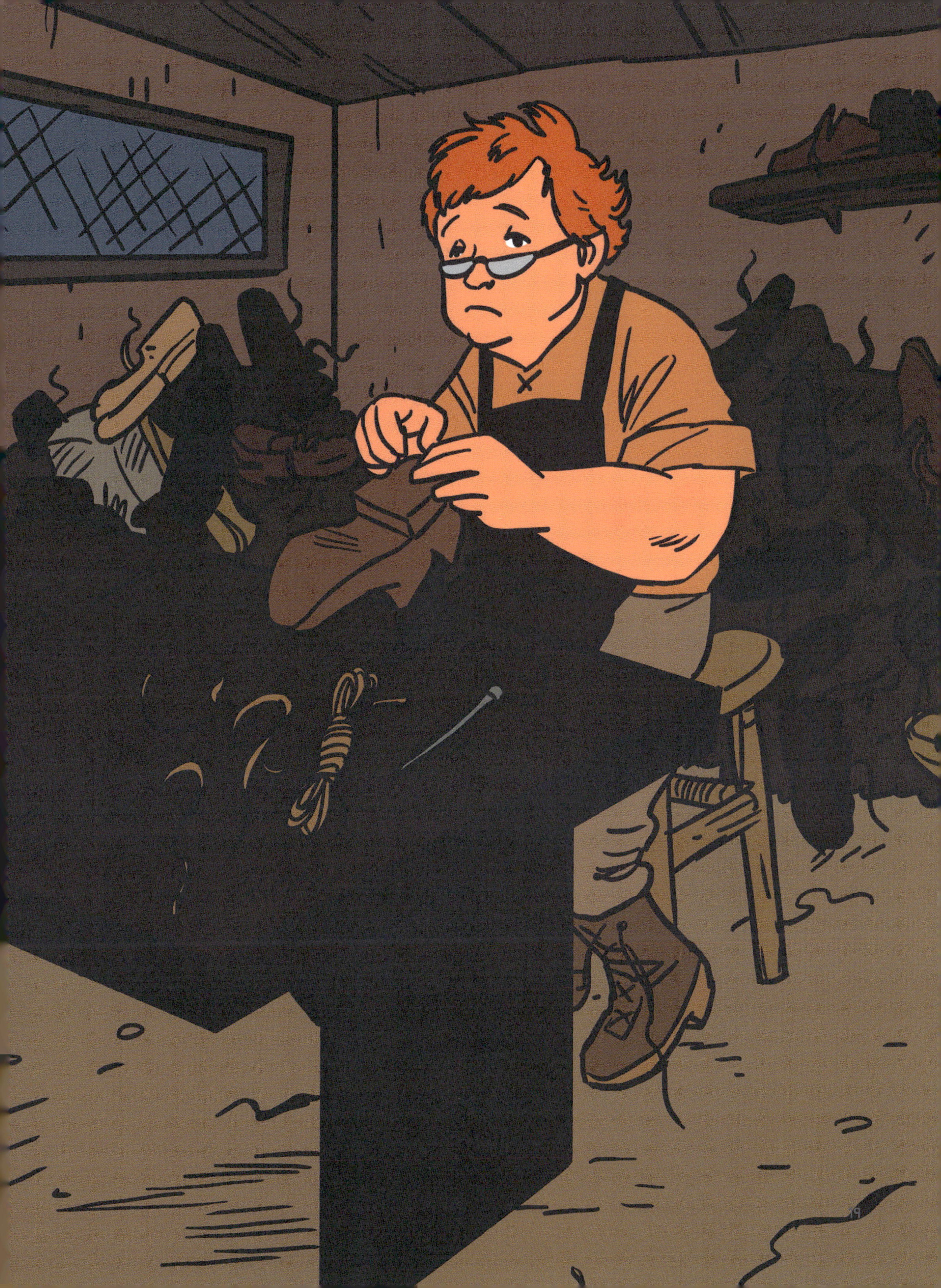

Brad Brogue he made shoes
But good – they were not
And try as one might
The laces to knot

        They still came apart
        And trailed on the floor
        So after a while
        People bought them no more

                So propped at the bar
                Where he drank for some fun
                The shoemaker's shoelaces
                Were always undone

So Merlin decided
Some help to provide
Delivered new laces
To where Brad did reside

        Where they had come from
        Brad did not know
        And to his surprise
        In the dark they did glow

And even more magical
Because made by elves
Once laced in the boots
They then tied themselves

        In beautiful knots
        Secure and real tight
        And to keep wearers safe
        They lit up at night

                The kids were delighted
                The parents weren't grumbling
                No more in the morning
                Were they fingering and fumbling

The sales of Brad's shoes
Rose like a rocket
And gold coins just tumbled
Into Brad's pocket

            And soon he adopted
            Great airs and graces
            And pretended that he
            Had invented the laces

He did try to find
But in time less and less
The person to whom
He had owed his success

But at last he then wanted
the folk all to know
That he made the shoes
and the laces that glow

23

Snuggelltite was the name
Of this place of renown
Just three miles due south
Of Bethlehem town

        Where a census was planned
        In one year BC
        To find out who lived
        In the towns and country

                Tired travellers trailed
                All through Snuggeltite
                Looking for food
                And a bed for the night

And a strong pair of boots
To soothe tired old feet
And a well made wax candle
To light up the street

And if they had a cart
That needed repair
They were sure glad Tom Timber
Was resident there

        Or something to eat
        (We all need our food)
        So for Bill Boyle as well
        Business was good

                So the artisans prospered
                Made fortunes galore!
                But Merlin observed that
                They still wanted more

Poor pilgrims were charged
The very last dime
From whomever in town
They found themselves buying

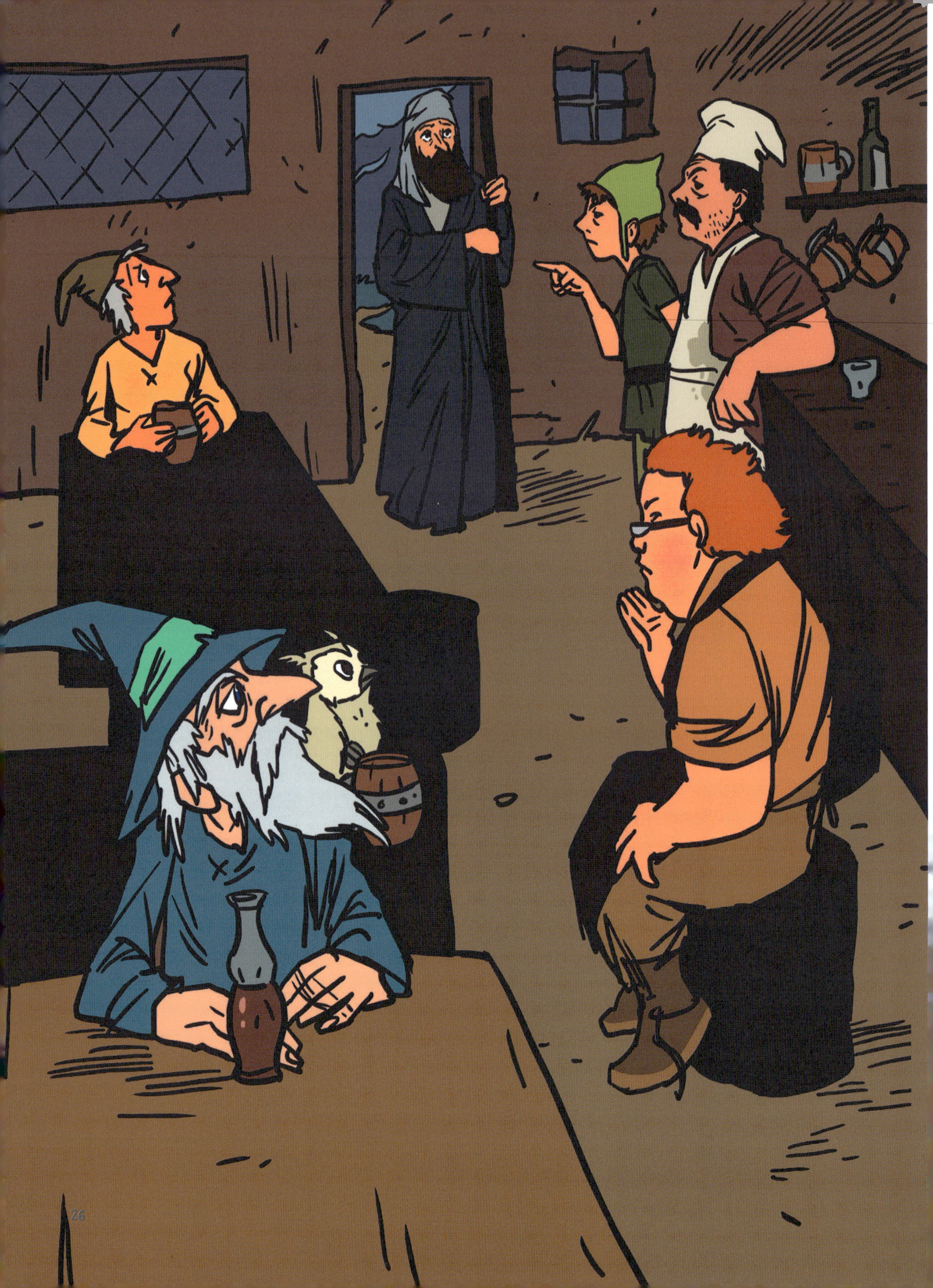

Then one Winter's night
Near the end of the year
Whilst the men in the tavern
Were supping their beer

        A poor carpenter came
        On a night that was wild
        And with him, his wife
        Expecting their child

                On a donkey she sat
                While he led the way
                Through the wind and the snow
                That on the ground lay

With the birth drawing nearer
And the snow piling higher
Joseph thought at the tavern
For a room he'd enquire

        He pushed the door gently
        And entered the bar
        Then the drinkers all stared
        At the man from afar

Covered in frost
From his head to his toe
Frantic with worry
With no place to go

        He told the innkeeper
        His wife was with child
        And they needed some shelter
        From the storm raging wild

                'I am sorry', he told
                The sad and tired stranger
                'The only thing left
                Is a dirty old manger'

'I'll take it' said Joseph
Without hesitation
Aware of the perils
Of their situation

        He spoke to the drinkers
        So merry and gay
        And asked for a candle
        To light up their way

Will Waxxel replied
In a voice that was gruff
'I do not believe
You have money enough'

        'Perhaps' he requested,
        'A pair of old shoes'
        But Brad said he needed
        His money for booze

                He said they were starving
                And prayed for a meal
                But Bill Boyle refused
                Any pity to feel

He then asked Tom Timber
If he might feel able
To give him some wood
To fashion a cradle

        Tom Timber just sneered
        'How could I live
        If I were to tramps
        My good wood to give?'

Joseph retreated
To the darkness outside
But still blessed those patrons
Who had wounded his pride

                But Merlin was angry
                At the drinkers did stare
                Found it hard to believe
                How ungrateful they were

                              And swore a great oath
                              To place into danger
                              The oafs who rejected
                              The downtrodden stranger

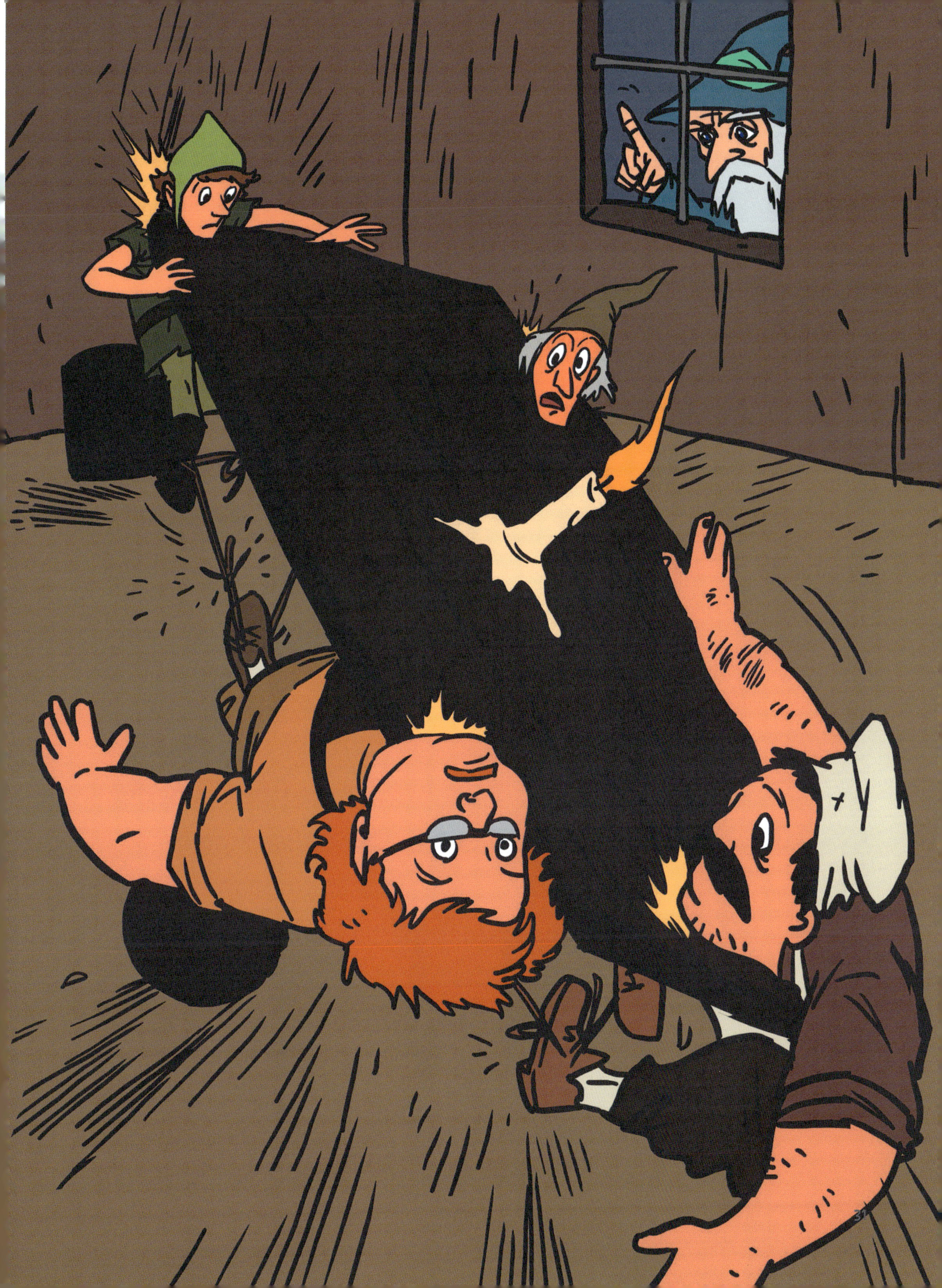

When the bar shut
And the drinking was done
The fools at the bar
Still wanted more fun

        So off to Bill Boyle's
        They all did retire
        For more of his burgers
        And drinks round the fire

                But Merlin he followed
                Them home to this session
                Determined to teach
                These rogues all a lesson

He reached the front door
And looked through a curtain
And when he was sure
They were all there for certain

        He pulled out his wand
        And then cast a spell
        to teach them a lesson
        and one they'd learn well

They were sat round a table
On Tom Timber's chairs
And as they were drunk
Were at first unawares

        That the table itself
        Had started to grow
        Like Tom Timber's wood
        As they sat in a row

                Eating the burgers
                Bill Boyle had just cooked
                They laughed at the stranger
                And how poor he had looked

The table grew longer
It simply expanded
And onto it's side
One of Will's candles landed

        They jumped up at once
        The fire to put out
        But as they stood up
        They all fell about

Their laces were tied
All to each other
Merlin knew all too well
How to cause them some bother

        They jumped up again
        All bruised and sore
        But, all tied together
        They fell down once more

                The fire was now blazing
                Totally out of control
                As all over the floor
                The drinkers did roll

Eight legs tied together
A great human spider
And but for a boy
They would surely have died there

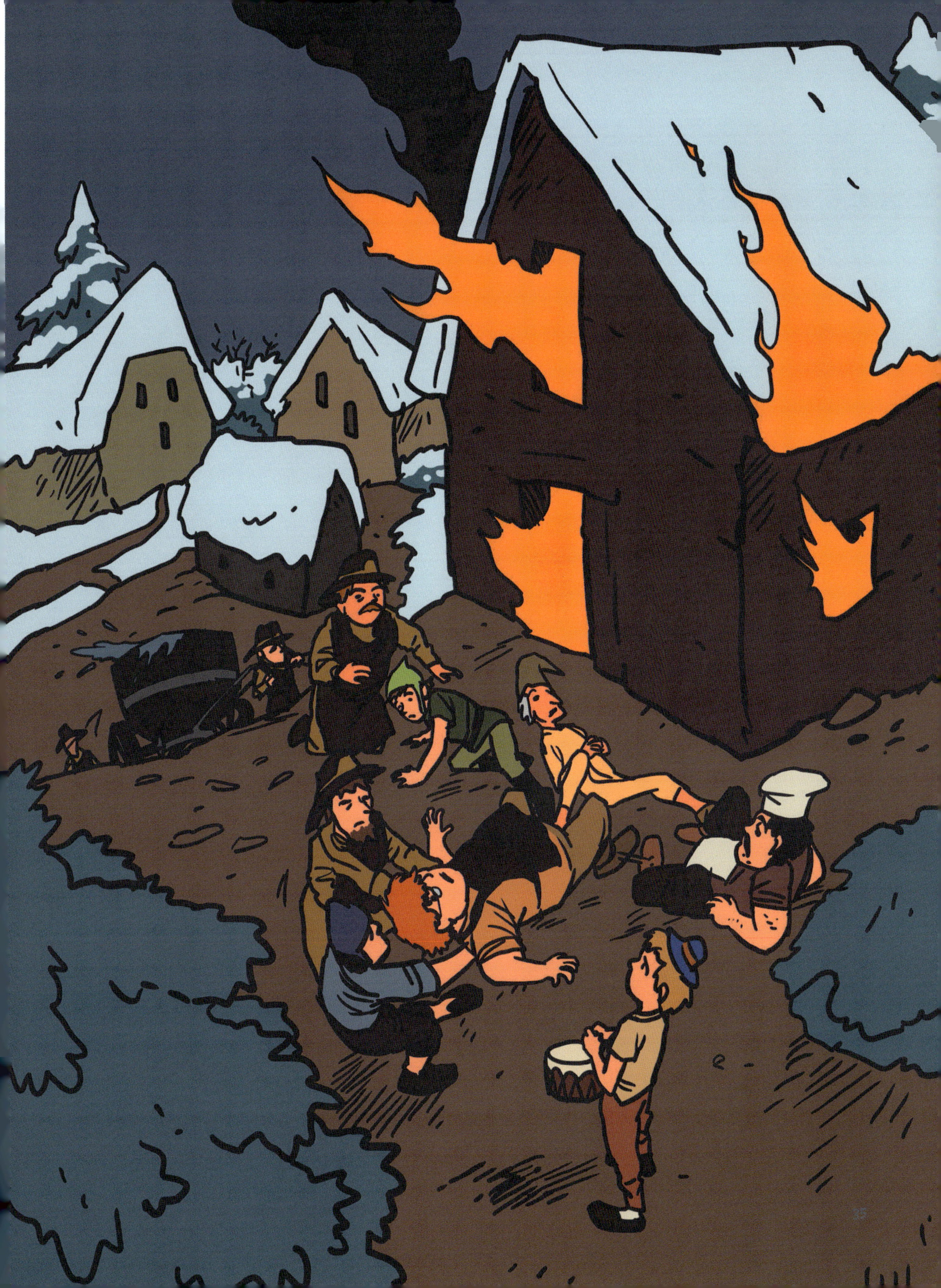

The child who arrived
Was a little boy drummer
Who'd come to the town
On his own, during summer

                No parents had he
                And his clothes were a sight
                But he played on his drum
                From morning till night

                              He spoke not a word
                              He just drummed and walked
                              And no-one was sure
                              If ever he talked

But he spotted the fire
And them frying like bacon
And drummed on his drum
Till the town he did waken

The firemen arrived
And pulled them outside
With little then lost
(Save for their pride)

        It was then that they tried
        To thank this poor lad
        For the real close escape
        That they had just had

                But though he remained
                Ever silent and dumb
                He beckoned to them
                To come follow his drum

And the drummer they followed
Who'd saved them from danger
Until shortly they reached
A dirty old manger

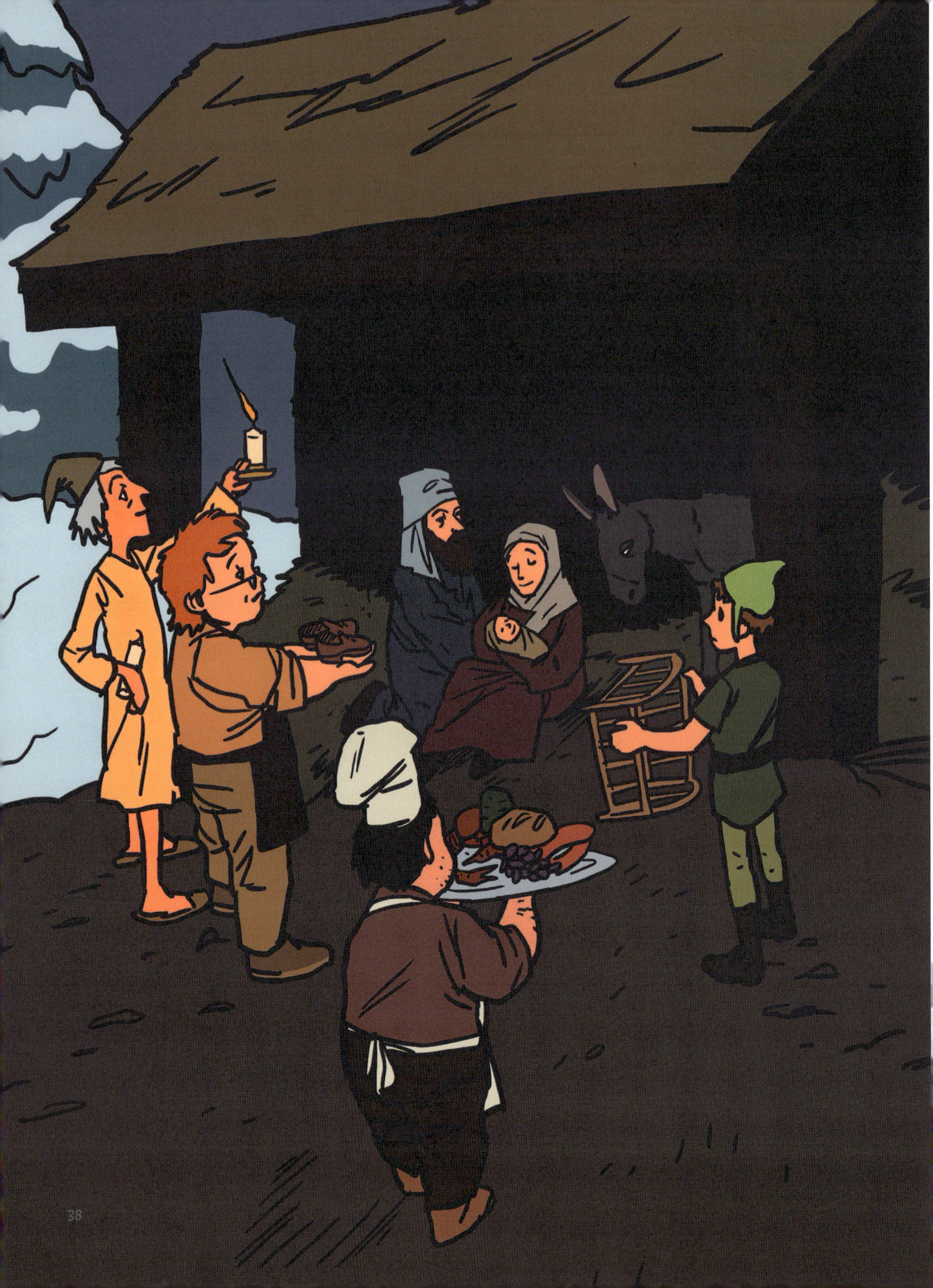

And when they reached
The stable door
The drummer stopped
And drummed no more

        Inside they heard
        A donkey bray
        A gentle voice
        Which then did say

                'My dear Mary
                do not fret
                our baby child
                is not born yet

and as we know
the Lord is good
and will provide
us soon with food

        And if the darkness
        We can't handle
        No doubt somewhere
        We'll find a candle

And if he can
As sure as not
By morning time
We'll find a cot

        And if indeed
        The Lord we please
        For baby's feet
        Some small bootees'

                And so outside
                This simple shed
                Amongst the drunks
                The guilt soon spread

For what they'd done
And what they'd said
To leave a babe
Without a bed

        Without a shoe
        Without a light
        Without a scrap
        Without a bite

So home they ran
At quite a pace
To compensate
For their disgrace

          But they returned
          Before the morn
          Just before
          The child was born

                    Will's candle lit
                    The manger bright
                    Tom Timber's cot
                    Was painted white

Bill Boyle's food
Was such a treat
Brad made shoes
For baby's feet

          And so when Mary
          Had her child
          The babe looked up
          And at them smiled

Just then the dawn
Anew it broke
And then the drummer
Softly spoke

              'I trust' said he,
              You appreciate
              Why I arrived
              In time, not late

                            If you thought that
                            strange or odd
                            It was not chance –
                            I was sent, by God

To save you sinners,
To set you free,
By giving you
An opportunity

                    To use your skills
                    To help those in need
                    To live in love
                    Not die in greed'

                                      So perhaps you've guessed
                                      As you kids are wise
                                      The funny old wizard
                                      Was but God – in disguise!

Printed in Great Britain
by Amazon.co.uk, Ltd.,
Marston Gate.